T0196320

TONES OF SADNESS ECHOES OF LOVE

A Collection of Stories and Rhymes

B.H. "RIEF" RIEFKOHL

authorHOUSE®

AuthorHouse™
1663 Liberty Drive
Bloomington, IN 47403
www.authorhouse.com
Phone: 1 (800) 839-8640

Published by AuthorHouse   01/20/2018

ISBN: 978-1-5462-1110-5 (sc)
ISBN: 978-1-5462-1109-9 (e)

Library of Congress Control Number: 2017915120

Print information available on the last page.

CONTENTS

ABOUT THE COVER

Like a waning sunset over the sea,
Life's moments do not last.
Eternity awaits, a hidden tear away.
How will you endure?
Will you be alone at the end?

DEDICATION

This book is dedicated to my loving family, my friends, to everyone I hold dear in my memories, and to anyone who strives to introduce others to the life-changing precepts, love, and power of Jesus Christ.

INTRODUCTION

Are you a player, a spectator, or a bystander?

"What is the name of the game?" the reader might ask.

Rene Descartes, the renowned logic-oriented mathematician, once said, "I am thinking, therefore I exist." Is the game merely existence? Is the game ordinary life?

The game my word pictures describe require the reader to go beyond the essential concept of logic. Join me in exploring the deeply hidden, psychological, spiritual, and emotional mysteries and truths of nature, love, life, and death. Unexpected benefits will result from your vicarious participation in my orations. As a player, I believe you will gradually become able to envision, feel, and discern hidden, essential concepts that many people do not understand. It is my hope this distraction from routine or reality will be strangely pleasurable and interesting for you. The intensity of future personal life storms may be lessened as you become more aware of your role in life's most important game.

Please turn the page, read, and play...

PALE YELLOW SUN

It always came at eventide
To seek me out, I couldn't hide
A herald bold of sadness won
The Devil's toy, pale yellow sun

When first it came in younger years
There seemed no threat, I felt no tears
Then life's long run began to slow
Pale yellow sun, I soon would know

The future comes, a shadow cast
And mortal pain began to last
Most battles lost with few to win
Pale yellow sun, came shining in

Life's pleasures gone, a heart to cry
The things I love within me die
Satan's sunset, has he won?
My sunlight ends, pale yellow sun

HOPES AND DREAMS

They said, "Dream big!" I said, "I'll try"
But youthful dreams can make men cry
I thought I tried with all my heart
In retrospect, I fell so short

So was it me or God's own hand
That guided fate to change my plan
Deep in my soul, I want to know
Why mental seeds sometimes can't grow

Fate deals the cards, we try to play
But fleeting time soon ends our stay
Each day I cry, what may have been
And sorrow reigns—a mind chagrinned

Someday God will take me home
The final path that's not our own

WHAT USED TO BE
WHAT MIGHT HAVE BEEN

What used to be what might have been
I hear a cry from deep within
And contemplate with cold chagrin
The broken dreams that love wore thin
What used to be what might have been

I run life's race and ride fate's wind
The sorrows now the pleasures then
A message God still tries to send
The bell tolls long to tell me when
What used to be what might have been

The days grow short God says to men
What is life and did you sin?
Will you lose or will you win?
Alone I wait to face the end
What used to be what might have been

FOREVER GONE

O, Reader—how shall I begin
To tell of wondrous things that end
And leave such sorrow deep within
What thoughts engage you when you hear
Of things now far that once were near
So many treasures we hold dear
Are part of us but disappear
All restless spirits seek the home
That once was part of us alone
Now ageless time still sings her song
The people, places fade like dawn
A last goodbye, a loving touch
An image gone I miss so much
These voiceless ghosts ride on the wind
Their message cold, a dying blend
Of joy and sorrow at an end
The hour glass of time runs out
The endless parts fall all about
And pierce this Player's heart in pain
And cry please call me back again
Each day Grim Reaper whispers low,
Why cry old Player, soon you'll know
The meaning of life's ebb and flow
I stalk old haunts, yet answers flee
Why can't things gone return to me

FACES OF LOVE

Long days ago, two hearts just met
A love there found, still lingers yet

Stay close o' things that once were thine
The hand of fate rewrites no line

Life's fleeting ghosts have hidden faces
Take care when love and hate trade places

Pull high your collar to face fate's wind
God's love in hearts will live again

THE SECRETS OF THE SEA

Timeless seas caress the shore
An ebbing touch a constant roar
A story told that few can know
How life began; when life will go

It stirs our soul
It cries, "Come near"
Eternal secrets you can hear
Our souls reflect the things we see
The earth, the sky, and things to be

Our hour glass of time runs dry
The song the sea sings, says goodbye
It draws us near one final time
We search for reasons in its rhyme

But life is gone each day we die
It never gives the reasons why
The rolling waves their secret keep
The ebbing tide makes death complete

DEVOTION'S SONG

Love's thread in life unravels slow
Devotion sings that we may know

A song of love that plays so long
It never ends when life is gone

A dog and man with bond so strong
I'll die within the day he's gone

When would we part, I couldn't know
How long he'd stay or when he'd go

In winter's night or in the spring
Devotion's Song, we soon would sing

The great outdoors, we both could see
But his eyes saw no one but me

The years flew by, it couldn't last
His strength was waning oh-so-fast

Dog's lives are short and man's so long
But still we heard Devotion's Song

Life's hourglass of time runs dry
Eternal sands hold reasons why

Devoted spirits never die
But stay entwined, no more to cry

When his time comes, he'll understand
Why he can't die in stranger's hands

I'll hold him close forever mine
Devotion's Song, death's bell will chime

He begged to go for one last time
This one who knew the hunter's rhyme

The failing gait the dimming eye
His trust still strong he watched me cry

Devotion's Song a last goodbye

I couldn't do it; love has won
How could I think this deed be done

He licked the hand that held the gun
Devotion's Song could still be sung

He looked at me, as if to say,
"You couldn't do it; it's okay.
We'll wait till nature has her way.
But please stay close, it won't be long."
Till then, I'll hear Devotion's Song.

One stormy night, he went away
I held him close till break of day

Two crying souls await the dawn
Devoted love is never gone

He looked at me and seemed to say,
"And now I go, but you must stay.
We'll meet again beyond the sun.
Devotion's Song for me is done."

My broken heart still feels the pain
I sit and cry love's tears like rain

Sometimes I think I still can feel
Those ears so warm—but it's not real

He haunts my dreams; soon I'll be gone
To sing with him Devotion's Song

Our song of love that never dies
We'll ride the wind and roam the skies

MORTAL FEAR

Life's little fears we face each day
They come awhile then go away
But fears exist that turn blood cold
And visit both the meek and bold
A plane soared high, he jumped alone
The fear intense cut to the bone
A brave bull's charge inside the ring
The snake whose fangs can strike and cling
Deep waters hold the shark's quick bite
Completely lost in cold dark night
We feel these things like in a dream
An elephant charge with piercing scream
The rifle blast, fear ruled the day
Why not avoid this deadly play
This inner voice can make men try
To feel this thrill and almost die
Such magic deep is sought by few
What do you hear inside of you?

THE SMELL OF DEATH

It flies the skies Grim Reaper's breath
It comes and goes and signals death
The nostrils flare to let it in
The smell of death rides on the wind

The Bell of Life gives its last chimes
I watched them die so many times
The glazing eyes, the choking breath
I knew they breathed the smell of death

The time for you is close, my friend
The Reaper says, "Invite me in"
Breathe deep and savor mortal fear
The final smell of death is here

DEATH IN THE BULL RING

It isn't fair, some people said
He had no chance, and now he's dead
With heart so brave and little fear
At dying gasp they cut his ear

Death's magic in the ring they seek
The people come and fill the seats
An unfair game, a brave bull tried
They weakened him until he died

A gleaming sword to pierce his heart
He oozed life's blood and played the part
This face of death the bull provides
Now matadors' cold fear they hide

A man could die, what is his fate?
Another death? The people wait
So many hope, a gleaming horn
Will find its mark, a body torn

What cruel things a mind can feel
Revenge and death can be so real
Cold hearts can lure us strange and far
And make us wonder who we are

To sense some pleasure at death's door
While bull and man may breathe no more

THE LAST WHIPPOORWILL

I heard a Whippoorwill last night
A pleading call that echoed fright
This night song spoke of sorrow long
No answer from a mate that's gone
Do spirits die in final pain?
A fading voice, a death refrain?
Some think that spirits live and die
And only few can hear their cry
A soul cries out; I am no more
I am the last and see death's door
I ride the moonbeam one last time
The final sorrow now is mine
And so a death song fades away
This singer sang his last today

WHEN LONELY RIDES THE WIND

When Lonely rides the wind
And only some can feel
The eventide and north wind songs
Whose loneliness I steal
The shadows call my name
A longing deep within
Comes back to haunt me one more time
When Lonely rides the wind

When Lonely rides the wind
All nature cries like me
Her tears fall on the dying land
Her death song's final plea
Why can't they hear her song?
All time will quickly end
When Lonely rides the wind

When Lonely rides the wind
Its call will never end
Across the marsh, above the hills
Life's cold wind screams, it never stills
How can we know whose soul it chills?
When Lonely rides the wind

When Lonely rides the wind
My soul begins to blend
With echoes racing high
Of wild geese in the sky
The night wind hides the pain
A lone goose cries and slowly dies
Of loneliness in vain
Forever gone he sings his song
When Lonely rides the wind

When Lonely rides the wind
It tells my soul to weep
A love no longer here
A promise I can't keep
My heart cries out within
When Lonely rides the wind

When Lonely rides the wind
A final time it tries
To cross the endless space of time
Then fades in darkened skies
Pale horseman come, the blood runs cold
You can't go home again
Alone I fly the endless sky
Like Lonely rides the wind

THE WILL TO LIVE

Remember when you still could see
All future things that still might be
But now a time in life comes near
The future starts to disappear
The will to live begins its wane
A journey made to stop the pain
Of things in life that hurt so deep
We move toward eternal sleep
The good times seem to fade away
Old memories cling but who's to say
When death will come and rule the day

LOVE'S CARING SONG

I'm just a dog, the people say
But I know hearts that came my way
A brutal kick, a loving glance
If only I could have a chance
To taste man's love and once run free
And hear a caring song for me

In cruel hands, I did abide
Chained to my house each day I cried
With little food and water there
I waited long with none to care
The freezing nights, the burning day
If only I could run away

And then men came with death's intent
I didn't care my last lament
My hopes grew dim, I heard one say,
"The dog pound's full, he'll die today"
"I just can't do it," one man said
"He's better loose than lying dead"
He cut my chain; away I fled

The winter wind blew cold and strong
I shivered days and nights so long
I searched and waited all in vain
A broken heart out in the rain

I lay there dying in the street
All passed me by right at their feet
The chill in hearts men never see
But dogs can sense the things to be
Cold death crept near; my wait was done
My caring song had not been sung

In children's hearts all love is pure
And caring songs can there endure
A voice said, "Daddy, help him please.
If he stays here tonight, he'll freeze!"
My hungry soul would soon be fed
I licked the hand that held my head

Each day I hear my caring song
It sings of love that lingers on
Beyond this world where spirits meet
On cold, dark nights in lonely streets

DEATH BY THE ROADSIDE

The bodies crushed the glassy eyes
No one to hear their final cries
On roads they died these creatures small
And nature weeps and mourns their fall

But human kind seem not to care
The roads run red with blood to spare
Relentless speed some place to be
With hearts so cold they cannot see

The writhing carnage left behind
In final death the buzzards find
To pluck the eyes and tear warm flesh
While some still live or death is fresh

God's creatures mourn like you and I
No sadness shown but hearts still cry
They search and call, but no reply
From those we killed or left to die

I hope someday we listen in
To hidden cries and try to blend
With spirit sorrows on the wind
But careless acts of man go on
While nature sings her saddest songs

WIND SONGS

Eternal songs still ride the wind
But only few can listen in
So many songs are there to know
And like the wind, they come and go
A true love lost, our mortal fears
A ravaged earth, a sea of tears

Here nature sings her saddest songs
A Whippoorwill that cries till dawn
The lone goose pleads in midnight skies
The sorrow echoes then it dies
God's creatures seem to understand
The wind songs speak, why not to man

The unnamed opus fills my soul
A story message dark and cold
It speaks to me, few others hear
Grim Reaper's breath is faint, but near

Soon music riding on the wind
Will have my sorrow blended in
When my time comes, I hope to see
Why life's sad music played to me

THE WHIPPOORWILL OF DEATH

I heard the Whippoorwill of death today
The hour is late, soon breaks the day
The ever-present question why
How long is life and who will die?
When will he come? When will he stay?
I heard the Whippoorwill of death today.

So sad his call; I know he weeps
He's so alone—he never sleeps
Life's promise made it never keeps
Each mournful cry calls me away
I'll soon be gone too late to stay
I heard the Whippoorwill of death today.

He calls his mate but no reply
Alone He waits and wants to die
When our time comes we'll be alone
The smell of death will linger on
Life's hopes and dreams will fade away
I heard the Whippoorwill of death today.

IF ONLY HE COULD GO

Few only seem to understand
The saddest part of Nature's plan
All wild hearts know until their end
The pain that's caused by wicked men

The wild goose captive stands alone
Like autumn leaves he should have flown
He hears the cries in moonlit skies
A mournful song and so he tries
To fly again, but fate denies

A saddened mate on high awaits
While he remains below
His silent tears span all the years
If only he could go

A soul that cries and slowly dies
A wild thing kept for show
No more he flies the endless skies
If only he could go

And Nature's song made man go wrong
For still another time
A broken heart within him beats
And slows each day I know
He looked at me as if to say
If only I could go

An answered plea, I set him free
As north winds took him high
A night song whisper called his name
I heard this distant cry

You set me free, but it's too late
My world has passed me by
Life's song is just a whisper now
And sorrow fills the sky

Your human heart within me beats
And slowly breaks with mine
Our final flight is oh-so-near
We share eternal time

Two souls entwined
That ride the wind
And still sing Nature's song
While men below refuse to hear
Life's music gone so wrong

I hope someday to understand the wild tides' ebb and flow
And be a part of Nature's heart
When it's my time to go

I'LL WAIT FOREVER
(A Dog's Lament)

A dog and man can have a bond
That lingers here till one is gone
Apart it flies where spirits go
And haunts each soul to kill them slow

When man leaves first, a dog will try
To understand the reason why
Their promise says we'll never part
He'll wait with beating loyal heart

Eternal days and nights grow long
A dying soul waits on and on
My wagging tail would say it all
O please come back you are my all

My hour glass of time runs dry
I wait and wonder if I'll die
Will life without you never end?
I hear your voice upon the wind

Your warm hands touch my ears again
I lean my frame against your skin
A dream for now, but soon we'll meet
A promise made, once more complete

THE PERFECT TIME TO DIE

The Alpha and Omega's plan
Still rides the wind and speaks to man
A hidden thing we try to know
When will our life blood stop its flow?

When will Grim Reaper come and say
Your time is here you'll die today?
No need to plead or run or cry
Life's curtain falls, it's time to die

We search for reasons in our realm
The death ship sails, who's at the helm?
Can our life's numbers give a clue?
Will Good or Evil come for you?

"Take number six," the Serpent cries
A cross shows seven; Jesus dies
The seven and the six combine
To make an age for dying time

If only one more year could pass
A double seven here at last
My thoughts rise up toward the sky
I've reached a perfect time to die

AND YET I STAY

I stood observing in my youth
And searched so hard for death's dark truth
Pale Rider came and took away
So many close went death's still way
I watched it all
And yet I stay

Life's sorrows flow like rising tide
And many take their final ride
The pale horse waits for me today
I feel his breath
And yet I stay

The reasons why are seldom seen
By those who never dare to dream
The dreams that seem to show men how
To reach beyond the here and now
To see a meaning far away
And give the answer why I stay

I hope someday my dreams reveal
The code of death so I can feel
Why others die and fly away
To meet their fate
And yet I stay

Fate's deadly mist now pouring rain
I cry, "Please take me home again"
I miss so much that was back then
So many lost that I called friend
Now shadows search for me today
The past retreats
And yet I stay

So now I wait with sorrow nigh
To look cold death straight in the eye
And say to him, "Why this delay?"
Most all are gone
And yet I stay

God's plan remains, when all is gone
Grim Reaper acts not on his own
But waits to hear what God will say
The message comes
And yet I stay

TOO LATE TO CRY

Life's music plays
Each day we die
A song so short this lullaby
Bold dreams are gone
Why did they fly?
The field lies dead
With rows laid by
Old tears well up
Too late to cry

We stumble on like living dead
But it's too late the Sweetheart's wed
Fate shows her shroud
Dark turns the sky
And it's too late
Too late to cry

A message sent that can't be read
If we could know
Just what it said
The heart grows weak
The dimming eye
Life's wounds are deep
O 'Samurai
The death knell sounds
Too late to cry

The wind of death within us blows
We almost see what no one knows
How many times we wondered why
The pale horse rider rode so nigh
And now we sing our final song
No longer death will pass us by
And it's too late
Too late to cry

REINCARNATION

Our fleeting time together here
Soon slips away, a thing we fear
But God's world holds some secrets deep
Could there be more than quiet sleep?
Our logic says just let life end
Death takes away both foe and friend
Earth's changing forms are God's delight
We go away, return we might
As spirit things to live again
And once more feel what might have been
Life bonds are strong, when will they end?
Can things that were return again?

A VOICE FROM THE SALT MARSH
(An Old Duck Hunter Remembers)

It was a sound like no other, a whisper that came on the wind. Mother Nature herself was talking and only a few could hear, and fewer still could understand. The Labrador Retriever heard. You could see it in his glistening eyes. If only he could talk. For some reason I was one of those who could hear and understand. The voice always began, "Come near to the salt marsh and listen with the instincts and soul of a hunter. Be still and you will know what was, is, and shall be in this place."

If you are one of those from the past, think back and imagine you are there and remember. Listen again, as a Blue Norther howls across the marsh. Even the shore birds hear the voice and are silent. Again, be a part of the loneliest place on Earth. Relive the magic. Listen as the whistle of Pintail ducks in the cold, dark sky speak to your hunter's soul.

Hear the Lycoming aircraft's engine roar to life and watch the airboats' exhaust belch blue-orange flame into the freezing, black night before dawn. A moaning outboard motor leaves a wake of glowing phosphorus in the freezing water. Can you see it? Feel the airboat slide across the mud flats, parting the ebony clouds of ducks.

Again, see them rise off the edge of the shoal water, only to glide on cupped wings to the waiting decoys. Relive the raw excitement as thirty Redhead ducks are pulled toward the decoys as if they were tied to a string. Smell the pungent odor of spent gunpowder floating on the morning air. Listen as a string of greater Canadian geese plead their call in the distance and a solitary Plover cries out somewhere in the high clouds.

Think back, old friend. Were you ever a part of this and have you ever heard the voice?

Time grows short for the old duck hunters and time is running out for the marsh, herself. The great clouds of ducks are gone now and the voice that spoke to us is almost silent.

Mortally wounded by the presence of too many people, the salt marsh cries out in agony: a final plea to be left alone. The voice is less than a whisper now. My tears mingle with her salty blood.

I saw my son gazing into the cold gray sky of the last hunting season. I know it's in his blood. He knew he had to have a painting by the wild-life artist, John Cowan, but he doesn't know exactly why. I hope he can hear some of what I have heard and feel some of what I have felt before it's too late.

How I miss that place and the magic of that voice! If only we could return to those days and how it used to be. When my time comes, I hope I can take my last ride with death on some dark, stormy evening in winter. I hope my spirit will ride the screaming north wind, and just maybe, the voice will sing to me one last time.

ASHLEY'S SONG

Introduction

This is a true story about the life and death of a beloved dog, a story of requited love, devotion, and ultimate loss. Almost too sad to write.

I believe human emotions, like love and sorrow, exist between animals and man. I also believe they are transferrable and can be mutually felt. Ashley's Song is the voice of restless spirits seeking to rewrite the past and haunting broken hearts that whisper to each other on the night winds of eternity.

A little dog once came my way
Abused, neglected, thrown away
She looked at us and seemed to say
I'll do my best if I can stay
The miracle of love began
Of man to dog and dog to man
Then fleeting days and passing years
We always knew there would be tears
Soon age began to make its mark
No more long walks or screeching bark
Her eyes grew dim; she just knew dark
Our sorrow grew, her health news bad
We cherish all the time we had
I dug her grave out in the rain
With heavy heart so filled with pain
In just an hour she'd be slain
I could have stopped it if I tried

A death decision while I cried
The vet's cold needle pierced her leg
She looked at me as if to beg
If she could talk I know she'd say
I love you, take my pain away
But please don't cry; it's all okay
She raised her head to touch my hand
No greater sorrow felt in man
Love's last caress the final time
A dying heart so close to mine
Replace her no, I'll never try
She'll haunt my soul until I die
A deed of love, but still a crime
The guilt surrounds me all the time
With tears and flowers, I stalk her grave
And mourn the life I did not save
This sorrow fills my nights so long
I'll cry forever, now that she's gone.

WHO AM I NOW?

We search for reasons near and far
That whisper low just who we are
So many dreams that once were clear
Our driving force, we had no fear
Pursued and found, pursued and lost
We ran so hard and paid the cost
The hour glass of time runs low
Strange sadness comes and then we know
Life's meaning fades and sad winds blow
The things we love fate takes away
I killed my trusting dog today
Her memory clings each day I cry
And ask myself just who am I
To still that loyal beating heart
With love and guilt, I played the part
A cold grave dug out in the rain
Two spirits scream in mortal pain
A warm touch never felt again
Ask who am I that still remains
Now time goes on, my end is near
My life response no longer clear
Grim Reaper calls, I hear him say
"Who are you now? This hour, this day?"
He waits to meet me face to face
I'll never know the time nor place
Until that time just who am I?
A saddened soul, Lord hear my cry

YOU CAN'T GO HOME AGAIN

Fate says you can't go home again
Old memories fade like places then
The people gone cry in the wind
And whisper low, "Remember when?"
The fleeting years increase their spin
Can all that's past return to men?
I yearn, but can't go home again

Life's picture dims as I transcend
Death takes away the ones called friend
What love unsaid, my heartstrings rend
Can roses die and bloom again?
With no return where will it end?
I cry, but can't go home again

My being moans, "What price is sin?"
Hearts fill with tears and cry within
Life's crimson thread grows frayed and thin
One brief return and then I'll win
The longing slows, we near the end
Fate sends its message on the wind
A dark, cold grave says, "Now my friend"
At last you will be home again

FINALITY

I think about it now and then
My funeral time with friends and kin
When will it come, the time draws near
Grim Reaper's blend of tears and fear

A casket cold awareness gone
I sleep while others carry on
A pre-planned show, a short goodbye
All meaning lost for us who die

How strange to think about a time
When all life's treasures fade with rhyme
A plan for dying rules this day
My love remains, I've gone away

HOPE BEYOND THIS LIFE

We hope to win in all we do
The bell tolls now and it's for you
Beyond this life two players wait
The Devil's team knows sin and hate
But Jesus' team knows only love
So join while here to play above

POST SCRIPT

So now, what is your answer to my original question? Are you a player, a spectator, or a bystander?

Before you answer, there is now another game you must consider— one that involves your life, death, and infinity. I hope at this moment, you will decide to become a player on the team of the greatest coach and player the world has ever known. Read His book and seek the absolute, ultimate reward He freely offers. Unless you accept what I am telling you here and now, you will be a spectator or bystander with a deadly fate for all eternity. Make no mistake—this one of a kind coach and player is Jesus Christ. His book is the Holy Bible, and the reward is eternal life.

And so, eternity relentlessly presents itself as the writing moment for this old player comes to an end. My farewell to you resounds best in the eloquent words of Omar Khayyam, "The moving finger writes; and having writ, moves on: nor all thy piety nor wit, shall lure it back to cancel half a line, nor all thy tears wash out a word of it."

I wish you echoes of love...

Rief

Printed in the United States
By Bookmasters